remembering
green

For Pat and Mickle – thank you
for all the laughter and love

Text copyright © Lesley Beake 2009

First published in Great Britain in 2009 and in the USA in 2010 by
Frances Lincoln Children's Books, 4 Torriano Mews,
Torriano Avenue, London NW5 2RZ
www.franceslincoln.com

A catalogue record for this book is available from the British Library.

ISBN: 978-1-84780-114-2

Set in Wilke LT

Printed in Singapore by KHL Printing Co Pte Ltd in September 2009

1 3 5 7 9 8 6 4 2

remembering green

lesley beake

FRANCES LINCOLN
CHILDREN'S BOOKS

Stolen

They came when the moon was dark and there were no stars. The wind blowing from the desert covered the sound of their camels and their muffled calls.

They came through the palm trees beside the river and their eyes glittered above the black cloths wrapped around their faces. They came when we were asleep.

They stole me while my mother and my brother slept – and the new baby, lying on the lamb's fleece. Nobody heard them because they were swift and silent and deadly – and they knew what they wanted. They wanted me.

They knew where I was because somebody told them. And that was worst of all. On the long, terrible journey south to the Drylands, that thought stayed in my head: somebody had betrayed me.

They took Saa too.

Chapter One

'Right. Next?'

Sharon moved her gum from one side of her mouth to the other. 'Two brown slices and a red vegetable,' she said.

'What?'

'Two brown slices and a red vegetable!' Sharon was irritated, I could tell. Sharon often was.

The woman serving looked annoyed.

'That'll be three carbon credits,' she said grumpily.

Sharon tossed her shiny yellow hair over her shoulder and winked at me.

'It was only two and a half CCs yesterday,' she said.

'It's warmer than yesterday,' the woman said nastily. 'Three species gone since Friday, they reckon.

Brown slices cost more.'

Sharon considered. 'And the red veg?'

The woman smirked. 'Same thing, really,' she said. 'Everything's getting dearer – dear.' She laughed. 'It's all right for you rich kids. Some people haven't seen a red vegetable, never mind a brown slice, in years.'

Sharon fingered through her wallet and found the carbon credits. But her mouth had a sullen twist to it that didn't augur well for the rest of the afternoon...

⠶⠶

Sharon is the only person here who is friendly to me – sort of – when it suits her. I have been here for just four moons, although it seems like years, but the others still look away when they see me, won't catch my eye, won't smile at me. Sharon does, sometimes, even though she is a Tekkie and Tekkies have another kind of life. One that has a lot to do with beeping machinery and small flashing screens and signals telling them when to recharge their ion extractors or plug in their enhancers.

The rest of us just get on with it, here on The Island, putting up with the blinding light that reflects endlessly off the pink sea and the warm wind that blows – and blows and blows – from the south-east most months of the year.

Once, Sharon let me go with her into one of the chill chambers – just for a minute – so I could feel what it was like. It was strange in there and I wasn't sure if I really liked it. Tekkies lay around on smooth plastic couches and the light was dim and soft. Air that was so cold it was white came chilling out of the vents in the walls, swirling in front of the lights and dampening the sleeping Tekkies who lay there with their eyes closed and smiles on their faces.

I was only there for a short time, and yet the hairs on my arms prickled, and I shivered. It was too dark – too cool – not real. And although the blast of heat and bright hit me like a stone when we stepped outside again, I welcomed the warmth.

For a moment, just for a moment … I remembered another kind of cool. The cool of river water and cold stones, the cool of black shade on hot afternoons, the cool of a palm leaf fanning gently; the cool of a hand on my forehead and the cool of my mother's voice…

My mother … will I ever see her again? Sometimes, when I let my mind go to the place where she lives in my memory, I ache with the dull pain of losing her.

We didn't have all the things the Tekkies have – no music coming out of little silver boxes, no pictures from earlier times coming out of glass tubes, no temperature controls and comfort switches.

Instead, we had the sound of the wind in the palms beside the river. We had the stars overhead at night, clear and silver and cool in the black sky. We had the comfort of a wool blanket when the nights were cool and the chill of river water on warm skin when the days were hot.

We had no walls and fences around us, no guards and patrols with snarl-fanged dogs. But we had each other. And we had a memory of times long gone and the stories of the elders and the sound of laughter – and people smiling in their hearts.

I was born when the Earth was old. When I was born, there was a scent of rain on dust, the dust of Africa. And that is what my mother called me: Rain.

I think about my mother. She was tall and slim and she wore a green cloth swept up around her hair and a skirt where parrots flew in jungles and the sky was blue.

'Remember this,' my mother said. 'Remember this day.' I didn't see what was so special about that day. It was just a day like any other. But I listened to what my mother said, because I loved her. I paid special attention to the things that were ordinary that day, that were just as they had always been.

These are the things I remember:

Our house is in a village where palm trees grow and there is shade to sit in. In the day, when the sun is high, nobody walks about in the hot dust – that is for later, when shadows slip across the ground like spilt ink and the women laugh and shake their skirts and start preparing food for their families.

Then the children play and the boys have a socc-ball match in the bare patch behind the kraal where the milk animals live, and we girls collect our water pails and walk down to the river, balancing them on our heads.

That is the easy part, walking down. We laugh and skip and sing and tell stories. And when we come to the river, we dip our feet in the coolness and sometimes, if it is not too late, we swim, and our laughter splashes across the sun-soaked, brown water like stars.

Walking back is harder, with pails filled and the weight heavy on our heads, but we stand tall and proud, as our mothers and sisters have taught us, and carry the precious water back for our families.

Then we eat, all of us together in the hot, sweet dark that comes quickly in Africa, and we sit under the stars and our grandparents tell stories to the children, and everyone listens – even the older boys who pretend not to. Then at last we go to sleep, one by one, and the village is quiet until the next day.

How did my mother know? How did she know that soon would come the end of everything? Everything would change and the most important thing I would still possess would be the memories in my heart.

Chapter Two

Sharon was calling my name. 'Rain? Rai-ain!' she was whisper-shouting. (Nobody yells on The Island. It isn't allowed). 'Rain!'

I was back on the hard deck, with the hot metal under my stretched-out legs and the glitter of the sea blinding me. And I was thinking that my mother had asked me to remember that day just before my grandmother came home.

'Sharon,' I said. I wondered again why she was so interested in being my friend. And that memory … that moment … faded and I could not focus on why Grandmother's homecoming had unsettled me.

'Come *on*!' Sharon hissed at me, quite close now and looking angry again. 'We'll miss the Stravanga!' She was so close to me, I could see the gold flecks in her light blue eyes, but I couldn't see what was in her mind.

I wasn't too bothered about missing the Stravanga. It was boring watching Tekkies trying to pass the time. Nobody ever sits still on The Island, they are always busy doing things, things that mean nothing – but which make the hours pass until it is time for them to lie down in their air-chambers and rest, swallow their sleep-capsules, compose themselves calmly in their bunks and switch off.

I don't want to be switched off. I want to…

'Rain!' Sharon was shaking me now. She doesn't like it when I 'go away', as she calls it. It frightens her.

So we went to the Stravanga.

One of the older Tekkies – about fifty summers old – was in charge. He was very excited about a new, so-called 'imaging concept' he had developed, one that would make it possible to filter the Sun's light and produce something more restful and gentle.

How far is all this going to go? They already have things to protect them from just about everything uncomfortable or unpleasant – or real. Their food smells of nothing and tastes of hardly anything. Even the air inside is changed into something else, and the Tekkies, well … they are hardly people at all.

They are so smooth and sleek, smelling like artificial things made of seaweed, quiet and always calm.

But not Sharon. There is a little thorn pricking Sharon. Her strange, light eyes are restless and looking, always looking for something. Maybe that's why she chooses to be friends – some days – with me, an outsider.

The entertainment was just beginning (glitter dancers on helium tubes and boys playing their New Music on stratified omcorders). Sharon was leaning forward in her seat, her eyes fixed on one of them – Nam. She wanted him to notice her.

I slipped out of my seat, out of the Stravanga Dome and into the night.

At night the sea is gentler and the light quiet. A silver moon turns the hot pink of the water into violet for the dark hours, and the temperature drops. Even the metal casing that protects The Island from the sea is cooler.

Once – a hundred summers ago – this island was not separated from everywhere else. Once it was a mountain with a flat top, a mountain down at the tip of the continent of Africa, and the stone stood solid behind it for a thousand days' walk, all the way to a different sea on the other side.

Once there was a city here that stretched away

over the rain-plains to the mountains that are now other islands. There were great grey roads sweeping like ribbons over everything, and the land was covered with man-stone.

Once there were people living everywhere, busy with their lives and worries, raising their families, going to work in buildings that are now under the sea, talking about 'the weather'. Once.

Now the hot sea glitters where the city was and, just over the water, so near that it pulls my heart, is Africa – where I come from.

Sometimes, on days when the wind blows from the north for a change, I can smell Africa. Here they call it 'Out', and they worry about it, looking over their shoulders as if there were something there waiting to pounce.

The north wind smells of dust and dryness and long nights trekking over the sand. It smells of my journey here on the camel train that snaked over the Drylands following the courses of old, dead rivers. It smells of the leather straps that they used to tie my hands and it smells of the old camel blanket they threw me at night when the desert chill struck. It smells of the path to my village and my family, and my heart. It smells of the way home.

Then I think of that night when I was stolen.

Strong arms lifted me from my sleeping-place as other hands stuffed a cloth into my mouth. I thought they were going to kill me, but they took me swiftly to the camels. There was hardly a sound, and the beasts' feet were noiseless on the ground. Someone tied my arms behind my back and made sure the gag was secure. Then I was flung on to a saddle and fastened there.

For a while I was so afraid, I could not think at all. I could hardly breathe and the cloth tasted of something foul and made me weak. The swaying of the animal under me and the texture of the ropes that held me were all that I could focus on – that, and thinking of my family.

Then I began to be angry. *Why* had they taken me? *Where* were they taking me? And my heart sank like a stone and I thought of Saa. How could I have forgotten Saa? Guilt flickered across my mind like flame. Tears of despair came into my eyes. Saa…

A little spark of memory came to me and I heard my grandmother's voice.

'Rain,' she said to me once, when I was afraid, 'you must stay sharp and aware. You must listen with every part of yourself and watch, and scent, and taste. You must find out everything that there is to find.'

So I did that ... and there came to me, faint in the wind of the camels' passing, the scent of Saa; the scent of lion.

·∴·∴·

It was a long, slow journey, that trek across Drylands. We rested during the heat of the day, travelling only at night when the heat was less intense. Sometimes the men had business with other people who slipped silently into camp. I was always kept hidden when this happened, and their voices never rose above a soft murmur. I did not know what they were doing ... where we were going or – most terrible of all – *why* they had stolen us. On we went, on ... to nowhere.

There was no water on the surface of the land, only sip-wells that the low-men dug for their masters. Water would be carefully drawn through a hollow tube into brass bowls that clattered at the sides of the camels when we were travelling.

If I rode one for a hundred years, I would never like the sway of a camel – nor its foul breath and its mean, spiteful eyes. When my head began to clear from the drugs they let me sit astride one, instead of being tied across the saddle. That was better –

but not much. Nobody spoke to me and I kept my eyes down. It was safer that way, although there was little to see of their faces behind the dark cloths they swept around their heads against the dust – just glittering dark eyes that never smiled.

Day after day we crossed that wide, brown, waterless land. Night after night I rolled myself in the dirty blanket and willed myself not to cry. There was nothing else I could do that could be called brave. My grandmother would not have cried. My grandmother would have stood straight and looked her captors in their mean, uncaring eyes and dared them to hurt her. I was not brave enough for that, but I did not cry.

And when I thought of Saa, I was brave. They let me take her a bowl of water and some scraps whenever we stopped, but her head flopped almost lifeless from the drugs they made me put in her water, and her eyes were dull and glazed. She travelled in a cage slung from a camel which tried to bite me whenever I went to her, and who rolled his eyes in fear at her scent.

I couldn't touch Saa. There was not enough space through the grid. The only thing that could reach her was my voice. I lay on the ground beside her cage and let my words surround her.

'Do you remember, Saa,' I asked her, 'the sound of the river? Do you remember how we used to go there sometimes when the moon was dark and there was nobody to see us? Do you remember how we climbed down the rocks – the small night creatures watching us with silver eyes, and the sound of the night hunting-birds, like ghosts in the stillness of the dark?

'Do you remember the cool water, the velvet of it? And the silvery bubbles and the small fish? Do you remember green – the smell of it, and the sound of new leaves shivering in the small wind?' Do you, Saa? Do you remember?'

And so our nights would pass on our journey to nowhere, Saa and I. She lay very still. Her ears hardly twitched and her great paws were lifeless – both of us were powerless in the face of this captivity. I would not run – our captors knew that. I would not melt into the darkness and disappear, not with Saa caged and broken. Saa was my life now. Saa was everything. I would die for her if I must.

One morning, as I woke from troubled dreams, I smelled a strange clean smell on the wind and at last we came to something my grandmother had told me of, although I had not believed her. There was a vast lake stretching along the land as far as my eyes could see. Its water crashed on to the sand at the edge of the country, white and frothing and dangerous.

It was the sea.

But grandmother had been wrong about one thing. The sea was not blue. It was a greyish-pink, like the rose-coloured stone my mother wore on a leather thong around her neck.

For three nights we followed the edge of the land, and the crashing and crashing of the water made my head spin. It was cruel water, salty and not fit to drink. The men laughed when I tried it. It was the first laughter I had heard for a long time. I did not smile in return.

And then we saw, glittering in the sun, The Island. Tall and steely-grey, it towered above the sea. Great metal plates bolted on to the rock held back the water that snarled and bit at its foundation. Sheets of shining glass towered high above the metalworks, polished and hard in the cruel light.

Then everything happened quickly. The cloth was tied around my head again so that I could not see and could hardly breathe. I smelled the sweet, sickly smell of the drugs and, although I fought it, a dull sense of losing contact with what was real.

And so I came to this place, this island, that was to be my prison, where nothing is as it seems and everything feels wrong.

Chapter Three

I sat still as a stone on the deck of The Island, remembering. And then some sound, some awareness bought me fully awake and alert and trembling. This was not a Tekkie voice. It belonged to somebody else from Out.

It spoke to me once more. 'Rain,' it said. And then it spoke again. 'Rain.' And the sigh of the voice was like a shadow, and my heart stopped still.

He stepped into the moonlight and I looked at him. He was brown, like me, but taller and slender. His skin was like the toffee that my mother bought for me once from a Traveller, when I was small – so dense and smooth, I wanted to touch it with my fingers. His eyes were shaped like almonds, black almonds, and he was smiling at me.

'Yes,' I said. 'I am Rain.' I did not know what else to say. He nodded, and took hold of my arm to draw me with him into the shadow again.

'You are one of us,' he said softly, 'and it is time for you to know who we are.'

It was dark out there on the deck, and very hot. The boy held my wrist lightly between his fingers, cool and strong. He led me swiftly between the shadows, slipping down a staircase and through a door that I had never seen before. In a bare room so small that it was almost a cupboard sat an old man – seventy summers, maybe. He smiled.

'At last,' he whispered. 'We meet!'

I bowed my head. He nodded towards the boy. 'This is Ghau,' he said, smiling a little. Ghau inclined his head, his eyes never leaving mine.

It was very still in our small space. Ghau settled himself on his heels with his back straight against the wall. I stood, half-ready to flee. But the old man was not afraid. He spoke slowly and calmly. Outside, the beam of a searchlight swept over the sea, passing across us as it circled endlessly, lighting the dark suddenly and going restlessly on.

'I shall not be here long,' the old man said. 'We must waste no time, for there is so much that I must tell you.' He paused. 'Much that your grandmother would wish you to know.'

'Grandmother... you know my grandmother?'

'She is ... known to me,' he said, looking away for a moment. 'She is long known to me. We...' And then he seemed to think better of what he had been going to say, and sighed. 'It is so complicated.'

I must have looked frightened, because he smiled. 'There is no need to be afraid – now. They are busy with their ... *entertainments*,' His lip curled when he said that, and I thought about the glitter dancers on their helium tubes, and understood.

But I wanted to hear about my grandmother. Hearing her spoken of brought a warmth to my heart. I made myself concentrate on what he was saying – what she would have wanted me to hear.

'This island has many secrets. Perhaps it could not function if anyone knew everything about it. From the first, it was a place where only certain people could come.'

He looked up at me to see if I understood.

'In the beginning, when the ice began to melt in the far south and the farther north, and the sea began slowly to drown the land, people were chosen who had special talents. Scientists were brought here who could explain what was happening to the world. Great artists were invited from their homes so that their skills would not be lost. Writers were asked to record the process of change.'

He looked away for a moment, and his face was grim. 'I was one. I am called The Writer.'

He looked back at me, and there was a question in his eyes, but I didn't know the answer. After a moment, he went on:

'This was to be a good place, a fine place – a place of hope. But you can see that it is not. For there were those who watched The Island from outside and wished they were here. There were people of wealth who *bought* their places – and brought with them their husbands and wives and children and friends, and people who were useful to them.

'And, as time passed and the world became hotter and drier, there was a need for technicians to build the great metal walls protecting The Island, and to make and service the machinery that kept it cool. There was repair work to be done on the sea-plates and drains to be cleaned.'

The Writer's voice dropped, as if he could not bear to go on. 'There were guards needed to patrol the perimeter and stop others from storming The Island when the floods rose and the food was finished. There were brave souls needed to throw back the children who managed to scramble on to the sea walls when their families were gone. There was all this work to do, and it was not to be done by the people who called themselves the Tekkies. It was done by others.'

None of us spoke. I could not think of anything that would fill that terrible silence, but after a while The Writer went on:

'So now there are masters and servants, as there have always been; and there are people who are neither.' He stopped speaking and was quiet, considering his words. 'Like you. Like Ghau. And now you are both here. With the people of The Island there is always a reason for everything. They do nothing without a purpose.'

The Writer looked directly into my eyes then. 'Do not let your guard slip. *Ever!* Do you know why you are here?'

I still didn't know the answer to that. 'Am I here because of Saa?'

But he didn't answer my question. His voice was gentle, a whisper. 'Tell me about Saa,' he said.

'Saa is … Saa is like … she is like the river, strong and free and filled with power. She is honey-gold, and her eyes are bright like stars and her fur under my fingers is like grass bending before the wind.

She is Lion – and I must keep her safe.'

For a long moment, he was quiet. 'But who are *you*?'

I looked back at him, and I did not know the answer. There were so many questions… 'I don't know,' I answered at last. 'I don't know.'

My eyes flickered over to Ghau, sitting silent and watchful, his eyes on the doorway, his whole being tuned to danger. Had he too been stolen? Why were we both here?

Ghau must have known what I was thinking. 'We are Rain Children,' he said quietly. 'We were born to the line of rain-makers among our two peoples.' He smiled. 'And now we need rain,' he added. 'We need it – and so do the Tekkies.'

'Do they think … they *can't* think that we are going to make it for them – can they?' Grandmother had never said anything to me about calling on the rain clouds. Never!

'Maybe.'

'But I can't … we can't! Or … can you?' I asked The Writer. He looked as if he knew everything. But he shook his head, waving his arm towards the door that led to the hot, pink sea and the ruined land.

'No.' He paused for a moment, as if what he

wanted to say was too difficult to put into words. Then he went on slowly. 'Long ago, there was an understanding of the land and the world – even of the stars and their movements. This was known centuries before Tekkies and their like came with shiny machines to make measurements.

'That understanding was lost long ago. Now the Tekkies only have measurements.' He looked at me. 'They long for that old understanding again. They long for it with a passion that dominates their minds and their thoughts. They think of little else. They *want* it! And because they can't make it… can't find it or invent it, they are going to try to take it.'

I thought of my journey here – the long hot nights, the queasy rag smeared with drugs to make me still. I thought of Saa. I nodded.

'Are you afraid?' asked The Writer.

'Yes.'

Then he looked at me for a silent moment, his eyes clear and calm, watching me.

'Are you ready?'

Ready for what?

I nodded. 'Yes. I am ready.'

Chapter Four

Ready. Not ready. Frightened half to death. I did not care about myself. I cared about Saa, and I knew what I must do: take her home.

Every moment of every day, I was afraid of what they would do to Saa, of what they would do to me. Every moment I wondered when they would strike from inside the soft skin bag of this place with their steel claws.

Sometimes, in the early morning, when I wake here on The Island and it is still dark, I think that I cannot rise from my bed and start another day. The fear in me is so great that I cannot make my legs move. I walk like a dreamer and my mind is stiff and unworkable. And then I remember that I am here because of Saa and that I must make myself function. I must do everything

I can to keep her from danger.

My people have always known lions – known them and respected them. In the caves near our river there are lion shapes cut into the rock, pictures that have been there for as long as any of our people. My grandmother took me there when I was a small child, whenever she had time to teach me our ways. The lion shapes seem to slide over the rock, ready to spring.

She saw my fear.

'It is your burden,' she said to me. 'It is your life-work to be the only one who goes between the lions and the people.'

But my grandmother did not know, I think, that my life was to bring me here, to this place that is not of the world, to this false land. She did not tell me that... and she did not tell me who I am. She didn't tell me anything about making rain, or understanding the stars.

Grandmother. Where is she now? How did they take Saa from her? Is she still alive? For a moment my heart stopped, I needed her so much.

It was quiet in our small space – all of us, I think, lost in other places and other times. Perhaps Ghau was thinking about me, because he broke the silence suddenly and angrily.

'You are Rain, Granddaughter of the River Woman, Daughter of the Lion People of the North, Keeper of Lion, Defender of Lion.' He stood up so that he was looking down at me, a head taller than I, and his eyes sparked. 'Did they not tell you?'

Then I remembered the times when my mother, or my grandmother, had half-said something and stopped. I remembered the kindness mixed with sadness. I remembered many things, and suddenly I understood. They had tried to protect me from this knowledge, to keep me a child for as long as they could. They had made me the gift of not knowing so that I could laugh and play and swim in the river with the other children. But in my heart I had guessed, and now I knew it was true.

'I ... I don't know what ... I must do,' I said at last, and my voice was very small.

'That is why I am here. To help you,' the old man said. His kindness brought water to my eyes, as the fear I had known for so long had not.

And that is how it began, my other life on The Island. That was the end of my childish time. That was the beginning of my strength and my work: to take Saa back to my people.

The old man spoke low and seriously, and I hunched at his feet, drinking in his words. For many minutes he talked, and his eyes never left mine. Ghau stirred from time to time. I didn't move a muscle.

He told me of the despair of the people who had once lived here, and of the slow rise of the water when it was too late to do anything.

'They knew,' he said softly. 'The governments all over the world – they knew a hundred years before, they knew that change was already happening. They knew that the way of their world was wrong, and yet they chose to do *nothing*. And when the change came, it came quickly, because the harm was already done. Year by year the sea levels rose and the cities by the sea were slowly drowned and all the systems they were so proud of failed.

'There are ways … ways that the Tekkie scientists know … to make water from air. They use a rare rock that Travellers bring them from all over Africa, when they can get it. There was water deep under the sea, too, and they found ways of bringing it to the surface and storing it deep in The Island – but only for their own people, not for others.

'Now the water under the sea is almost gone, and the rare rock has become even rarer, and the

llers find little of it – and what they do find is
nd price. The days of this island are numbered.
It cannot survive unless water is found – or unless
something happens to change the way of the
world. That is what Tekkies most desperately need:
change.

'And change is coming. Without their help or
need, change is coming, and they are powerless
in the face of it.' His eyes glowed in the shadow.
'There is a stirring in the land, and you and Saa and
Ghau are part of that change. It is late, very late.
The rain people have been peaceful and still
and hopeful of forgetting ... for too long. Now
change is here. It has come.'

He put his hand on my head and let it rest there,
heavy and warm. The three of us in that small space
were quiet and the silence was deep and powerful
and swirling, with dangerous currents going who
knows where.

It was Sharon's voice which broke the spell.
Why does she follow me so?

'Rain?'

We froze.

'Rain? I know you are there! I can smell lion!'
And she laughed softly. 'I *always* know where you
are. What are you doing?'

Slowly I straightened, my eyes still locked in The Writer's.

'Just … thinking, Sharon. Just thinking. I'll be there in a moment.'

'You're going to miss the nebulation contest,' she said. 'You *know* you enjoy the nebulators!' Her voice was a low whine, like a spoilt kitten. Why didn't she just leave me alone?

'I'm coming!'

'Well, hurry up, then. It'll be over, if you don't hurry!'

'My grandmother…?' I began to ask.

But The Writer seemed to understand.

'She is safe,' he answered quickly. 'Safe.'

Ghau bent close to me. I pulled my gaze from the old man's. The sweep of the searchlight flashed on Ghau's dark eyes, and for a moment I saw myself reflected there, frightened. His hand brushed my cheek and his breath was warm on my face.

'I am here, too,' he said. 'You are not alone.'

For a moment I looked at him. And there was no time for more of a farewell, as he turned me swiftly round and gently pushed me towards the stairs where Sharon waited.

Chapter Five

How can it be that nothing changes … and yet everything has changed? When I left Sharon and the Stravanga Dome, I was one person. When I sat down beside Sharon again, in time for the last of the nebulation contest, I was somebody else. And yet I still laughed at the show, still hoped the boy with the shadow-pipe would win, was still pleased for Sharon when Nam came over, seemingly by accident, and asked her if she was OK. (Why does everybody here always ask everybody else that? Do they have nothing else to ask?).

But inside me a new heart was beating – and in my mind were a thousand new thoughts. I had been asleep. My soul had been held like water in ice by fear and dread – and loneliness. Since they had brought me, and Saa, in the deep dark of a summer night, from the mainland of Out in a small boat that bucked and kicked against the sea like a captured wild animal, I had been imprisoned – not just in The Island, but inside myself.

I could see myself in one of the hundreds of mirrors they have here – they are always looking at themselves. I looked different, too – straighter, taller. I didn't look as ... beaten. I looked angry. Carefully I lowered my eyes, composing my face to be as it usually is. In future I would have to be aware of everything I did, watching myself in my own kind of mirror, reflecting back to them what they expected to see.

Tekkies are a mystery to me. Since I arrived here, I have watched them and puzzled over them and tried to understand them. Often they are sad. When they show V-Disks of scenes from the past, they watch fiercely, as if they could will back those times when everything worked – for them – and weather was something they just shut the door on. In those days, only poor people were affected when a wind blew fire through their settlements and rain turned their neighbourhoods into swamps.

For me, these old images are like a dream of something that never was real. They had machines almost everywhere, machines that could send messages and even pictures to anywhere in the world. They had what they called Stores of Richness where unimaginable wealth was kept. They had schools and colleges and places to teach their people everything they needed to know to keep their world safe. They had knowledge! How could they not have known how to use it?

My grandmother could remember some of these things from when she was young and *her* grandmother told her about them. She told me stories – at least, that was what I thought they were. Who could believe the things she told, when we lived as we had always done beside our river and our rocky hills, caring for our milk animals and growing the *tef* that was our food?

So now, while I moved around The Island, caring for Saa in the cool morning and the late afternoon, and carrying out my other duties during the rest of the day, I was thinking.

'What are you thinking about?' Sharon asked me. It was rest-day, the day that comes after nine working days, when everyone had a chance to stop what they were doing and breathe a little.

'Just … things,' I answered.

Her eyes flashed. This answer did not satisfy her. 'Tell me about your home. What was it like?'

My mind-eyes flew back to the deep shade under the trees and the sound of river, the sound of babies laughing and mothers singing.

'Simple.' I said. 'Not like here.'

'What did you eat?'

'*Tef*, mostly,' I told her, and smiled at her expression. 'It's not so bad – and it grows there. We bring water from the river to grow it, and we have milk animals and some bush foods from Wild.'

She shuddered. 'I've heard of Wild.' She looked frightened, but the good kind of frightened – rather like when something scary happened on a V-Disk, but you knew it was going to.

'There are wild animals there,' I went on, ' and above all, there are lions.'

She gave me a sly little glance. 'I would like to see a lion.'

Ah. Sharon would like to see a lion. Perhaps that's why she hangs about, waiting for me when I come from Saa, wrinkling her nose at the rank smell of cat.

'I have never seen a wild animal,' she added.

Suddenly I remembered, in a mind-picture, a day when Grandmother had taken me to gather bush foods. We were on the edge of Wild, not far from our village. Suddenly she held out a quick hand to still me and we stopped, quiet on the path, hardly breathing. A massive shape was moving across the track ahead of us, silent on huge feet. He turned his head to look at us, watching with his small, wise eyes, decided that we were no threat … and moved on.

'Elephant…' Grandmother breathed. 'The Old Ones.' And she turned round, and I followed, and we went back to the village without speaking of what we had seen.

I didn't tell Sharon. I didn't think she would believe I had seen one of the Old Ones. There are no animals here, not even dogs. There is no water for dogs, Sharon says, or cats. There are no milk animals grazing on the land on the other side of the sea either, no wool animals – nothing but dust and wind. Even in Drylands there are night creatures and insects and the sound of birds singing when the sun rises, and water in the sip-wells. Here there is nothing, nothing at all.

I could not bear to think of it. 'Tell me about you,' I said. 'Tell me where your family came from, when they first came to The Island.'

I think she had been waiting for me to ask. She smiled her little cat smile and smoothed her soft yellow hair. She answered proudly, 'My people once lived in the city that is now under the sea. They lived in a place called Round Bush and they had a home with lots of rooms and windows which looked towards the mountain that is now The Island. We were the founders of The Island. My grandfather was one of the first to see that it was needed, one of the first to make sure that his people would be safe when the sun changed and the sea rose.'

I tried this picture in my mind, but all I could see were old images from V-Disks that were like silver shadows of what once had been.

'My grandfather is a very powerful man on The Island,' Sharon added, and she was watching to see how I would react. I said nothing.

'Very powerful,' she repeated. 'He's one of the people who makes decisions.'

Powerful? Makes decisions? Decisions like sending Travellers to capture people? To capture me? To capture Saa? To take Saa away from Grandmother ... away from her place? And who had these important people spoken to, back in my village? Who had told them something I only half-understood myself? Who had told them about Saa?

Sharon was watching me closely. 'Would you like to know more?' she asked, and I wondered if she could read my mind. But the siren sounded for our meal-sitting, and we had to stop talking and line up with our trays and plates for red vegetables and brown slices. Sharon waved me ahead of her.

As I went, I could feel her eyes on my back.

Chapter Six

The night I first touched Saa, it was hot and fierce and a wind blew from the Drylands that dried out the small green *tef* plants and withered the land. My grandmother came for me, and silently signalled that I should go with her.

We walked along the small track that was not much used, the track to the caves and the lion pictures. A lemon moon shone steadily. We were quiet, not speaking, but I was wondering why we were going there. Then, when we came to the caves, my grandmother stopped, bent down and lifted something from a basket with a lid. When I stepped forward, she dropped it into my outstretched arms.

It was warm and heavy and full of strength and power. It bit me sharply on my arm so that I dropped it.

'Pick her up,' my grandmother commanded. I sucked at the blood from the bite, but I obeyed her – not just because everyone always obeyed my grandmother, but because I wanted to.

This time the animal had smelled my smell and was a little less fierce. She wriggled a bit, then settled into the crook of my arm and stared at me, bright-eyed.

My grandmother went on. 'She is quiet from eating the *bir* berries that I fed her. Next time, she will be wilder.' My grandmother laughed softly. 'Now she has had first-blood, you have a chance with her… Do not waste it.'

'What must I do?' I whispered. 'What must I do with her?'

My grandmother settled herself on a rock and told me to do the same. I sat – carefully – with the lion cub still in my arms. Her warm fur smelled of dust and wild and sun and she gazed at me unblinking.

'It is time,' my grandmother said. 'For long years there has been no Lion of Mpopo. There has been no Lion Woman. And look…' she waved her arm at the hot, dry valley below us, 'what that has brought us!'

'Her mother was killed,' she said sharply, 'for

her fur.' Her lips were stretched into a tight line and she was angry … angrier than I have ever seen her. 'For a piece of … *carpet*!' She hissed the word. 'Carpet for a foolish ruler in a foolish land!' She looked at me, her eyes blazing. 'And the hunters wrung the necks of her sisters because they could, and because it gave them pleasure. They missed this one.'

I looked down at the small cub. She had settled, heavy against me. I could feel her heart beating strong against mine.

'When lions are so few,' Grandmother continued, 'is it not terrible that their lives can be lost for such a cause? For a ruler's feet to tread on? To show off? For power?' She spat suddenly into the dust. 'Her mother's life, and the lives of her sisters – lost, for nothing?'

My arms tightened around the sleepy animal. She stretched and yawned, her sharp little teeth creamy-white in the light of the strange moon.

From that moment I was her – although she was not mine.

∴⁖∵

Saa was a secret – my secret and my grandmother's.

Although my mother knew, we did not speak of it. My job was to care for Saa and show her what she must do to be Lion. I must replace her mother and the other females who would have cared for her and pushed her away when she was too rough, and brought her scraps of food and let her sleep safe against their sides. I must be Lion, and I must do it well.

'There is no time any more,' Grandmother sighed. 'No time to plan, or think … or scheme. The time has come upon us and our actions now are what we shall be judged by.'

I did not understand, but I knew her words were important.

'You will stay in this place, with this lion, until she is grown – until she can return to Wild and find a mate… perhaps. This is your path.'

I bowed my head, my cheek against the stiff golden fur. This was my path.

•••••

Saa was strong. She hurt me often. But she learned her strength. She would watch me, her golden eyes staring, while I struggled. Everything was difficult – and dangerous too. Saa was only a few months old when she came to me, but she grew in strength every moon and she was a hunter, one who could kill.

It is hard to keep a lion. Grandmother saw to it that I had chickens – hard-earned food that would have supported people in the village – but she was determined. Much of my work was to look after the chickens so that Saa could be fed – bringing them water, finding shade for them; shaking out grain for them every morning before the sun was high. There were goats for Saa sometimes, that Grandmother killed quickly with one sure movement of her knife. Saa grew bigger and much, much stronger.

There was a fence. Grandmother and I made it and an old man helped us. Making the fence was hard. Saa was strong. The fence had to be checked every day.

I learned that Saa needed to play – and play, and play. I learned that I needed to be careful, always watching my back. She grew quickly and was always testing me. She allowed me to touch her. She tolerated me. She did not love me. But I loved her.

The day we let Saa run free for the first time is one I will never forget. We had some fresh meat from Wild to lure her back. Grandmother had told the hunters to bring it – and because they feared her, they had done as she asked. We hoped Saa would come back – but we did not know for sure.

We opened the gate of her fence-place. At first she hesitated, like a milk animal that is not sure if it is roped or not. But when she sensed her freedom, she ran out, and the beauty of her power was not something for words; nor was my terror that she would leave me.

For two nights and two days she ran, and I thought my heart had gone from me. I waited at her fence – and the time passed. The sun travelled once and travelled again across the sky, and still she did not come.

But on the second day, at evening, as I stood waiting with the fresh meat, she came back.

She took the meat and ate it, watching me with her great, golden eyes. And then she licked herself clean and looked at me some more. And then she walked on her cat-paws to where I waited, and lay down beside me, and the rumble of her sound travelled through my body and brain and became me – and she was Rain, and Rain was Saa. And from that moment we were one.

And so we lived. Saa grew. I learned. Chickens

hatched, chickens died. Goats came, goats went. But Saa, our lion, lived and grew...

Until the day when I went home to my family because my brother was coming of age. Grandmother stayed with Saa, and I went back to the village – and laughed, and danced, and smiled, while the sun set in the hot sky and the silver moon rose, and we slept the deep sleep of happiness.

Until they came in the night and stole me.

·ﾞ·ﾞ

'Can I see it?' Sharon's voice was sharp as the noon shadow, sly as a snake.

'See what?'

'The lion.'

I looked up at her. She was standing against the light, her hair blazing in the heat and the brightness. I was resting against one of the deck plates in shadow. It was hot. I was tired. Saa was hard work here too.

'It is not allowed,' I said quietly.

Sharon's eyes narrowed. 'But I *want* to,' she said. 'I know it's down there. I heard my grandfather talking about it to some of the other Lords when they didn't know I was around.' When I didn't answer, she went on: 'I can show you things in return!'

'What things?' There was nothing here on The Island that I wanted to see – except perhaps the way out of it.

'Anything. I know The Island better than anybody. My grandfather built it.'

This was not strictly true. The Island had been built by many people – Sharon's grandfather was one among many; but what *was* true was that the secrets of The Island were better known to him than they were to anybody else.

I was quiet for a moment, thinking. 'So… what things?' I said. 'What will you show me, if I show you something nobody here has ever seen – Lion? What will you show me?'

It was quiet there on the deck with the pink sea groaning and waves flecked with white smacking endlessly on to the sand far below us.

'That,' said Sharon, indicating the sea with a flick of her yellow hair. 'Down there. I know how to get there. To the beach,' she said. Her eyes met mine.

'It's the way back,' she said. 'The way to Out.'

Chapter Seven

Escape glimmered before me like hot air on a still day. I had often thought of it ... who would not? When the warm wind of Out blew through my mind, I longed for home with a sad, strong pain in my heart. It stilled me so that I could not think, could hardly move; almost stopped breathing. I tried not to remember my mother... my brother and sister; least of all could I think about my grandmother.

We shared something, my grandmother and I. Something that ran deep and true – and far back in time. Things that she said were like beads buried in sand. They led somewhere, if I could only string them together to make a necklace.

And there was Ghau. Where was he? Who 0was he? I was surrounded by secrets, surrounded by mysteries.

Before I could answer Sharon, one of the endless sirens sounded and she half-turned in obedient response, then stopped herself and turned back.

'Well?' she demanded. 'Are you going to show me Lion?'

My answer was in my throat and in my heart.

'Yes,' I whispered. 'I will show you Lion.'

Her smile, as she left, was one of triumph.

Saa was a prisoner in a space between decks where no Tekkies ever went. They lived their lives above, in the cool control of the silver machines, in the quiet of the silent gold-glass that held out the sun and the noise of the crashing waves. Down here it was hot, but the wind blew the land to us, making it real. Large gates barred the way to Saa, and there was a guard who dozed and grumbled until the time when his shift ended. The great plates of the sea-wall, massive and black, formed a barrier on two sides, and a strong fence of metal spikes held Saa back from the secret tunnel-ways of The Island.

It was dark. Light came through two high spaces in the sea wall, but not enough; not enough for my Saa. Her golden eyes had dimmed with the passing days. Her fur had lost its gleam and was dull. Sometimes she lay gazing unblinking at the small squares of brightness, and my heart twisted with sorrow for her. This was no place for a lion.

My tasks were clearly defined. I was to be companion to Saa for the hours of the day when I could be spared from my duties.

'*Light* duties,' the deck-keeper had sneered, when I arrived. 'So as not to tire you too much for whatever it is that you do down there!' This had not made me popular with the other captives who work on The Island. I had made no friends.

It was to Saa that I poured out my heart's trouble, while I cleaned out her bedding and put down fresh grass for her to lie on (who knew where the Tekkies got such stuff?) While I fetched clean water for her from the pipe-tap and cleared old bones from the meat they sent her every day (real meat, not brown slices), I talked to her of my sorrow and my longing.

And all the time, at the back of my small worry, was a big one. Why were we here? What did they want of us?

And all the time, in Saa's eyes was the question, *When are you going to take me home?* Yet another question to which I could see no answer.

Then, one day, while I was struggling to close the catch on the tap-pipe, I was startled to hear a voice. It spoke behind me and my heart stopped still.

'Rain,' the voice said.

It was Ghau.

I closed my eyes. The precious water from the pipe ran over my hand and Ghau laughed softly. He reached past me and his fingers, swift and warm, were on my hand.

'Let me,' he said, and the flow stopped.

When I turned to look at him in the half-dark, his eyes were worried.

'You are too thin,' he said, and his gaze switched briefly to Saa. 'And so is she.' Then he stepped back to see me better. 'Too thin, and too sad,' he said. 'But it is nearly time.'

'Time?' I squawked, like a frightened chicken. Maybe Ghau thought so too, for he smiled. 'Time,' he said again. 'You must be patient a little longer.' He glanced swiftly over his shoulder. Outside the gates, the guard was muttering that his relief was late, talking half to himself, half to me. They didn't like it down here in the heat, with the lion.

Ghau took something from his belt where it hung in a brown leather bag. When he handed it to me, his eyes were serious.

'It's a knife,' he said, 'It's small, but very sharp.'

I could feel the weight of it, and the weight of the danger too.

'Can you use a knife?' he asked.

'Yes,' I answered quietly.

'Could you use it against a human being?'

'For Saa, I would.' I did not add what was in my heart – that I would also use it for Ghau.

'And do not give Saa any more drugs. She must be clear-headed now. Start to give her a little less each day, until she recovers.'

I nodded.

We were silent, then we both began to speak at the same instant.

'Where…?'

'How…?'

Then we laughed, nervous with each other. 'You first,' Ghau said politely.

'I was going to ask, how did you come here? Were you stolen, like Saa, like me?'

He smiled. 'Of course not! The Tekkies don't even know I am here! I followed you!'

'*What?*'

'We are rain children,' he said simply. 'It was

my duty.' Then he smiled again. 'You saw no one following you while you were crossing Drylands? No one at all?'

'No one except the Travellers who stole me, and the men who came sometimes to talk to them.'

He looked pleased. 'I was there. I was with you almost from the beginning. I was on my way to you when they came.'

I was so surprised that I couldn't think of anything to say.

'And I was going to ask *you*...' But he never finished his question. One moment he was there, and then he vanished. Seconds before the gate inched open enough for me to be summoned, he was gone.

I wondered if our meeting had been real – or if I had wanted it so much that I had dreamed it.

But from that moment on I saw The Island with new eyes, seeing not just what was on show to be seen, but also the underpinnings, the structure where servants such as I were expected to be, where Tekkies never went.

At its core The Island was rock, solid rock. Once a city had clung to its flanks – I had seen that in the old V-Disks: white palaces of glittering steel and shining glass; ribbons of road snaking their way along a long-gone coastline; glass towers. Now the mountain was diminished, shrunk, but still it was the bastion of The Island around which everything depended.

High against the rock were the decks of the new city, flat and even, well-swept each day by underlings from Out, calmly paced by Tekkies deep in discussion of ... what? What did they talk about? Think about? Dream about? Were they immune to the worries that chewed at my heels like small, vicious, snarling animals?

Below was a labyrinth, a network, a life support veined and arteried by tubes and pipes, gangways and tunnels. Now that I was really looking, I saw servant people moving easily along these secret pathways, chattering to each other about the latest socc-ball match, fine-tuning valves and pumps, mending and welding ... maintaining the illusion of security that was The Island. No Tekkie seemed to know what was going on, or care. Each time I went to see Saa I explored a little further, pushing back the boundaries of my knowledge, storing information.

Now, when I whispered in her velvet ears as she lay with her heavy head on my lap, I whispered to her of escape. I told her of our path home and how we would cross the Drylands. I promised her the scent of river and the red earth under her great paws. I promised her the thrill of the hunt. Together we dreamed of the high skies and the thundering clouds of late afternoon – and stars … the stars … clear against black, black skies. We dreamed together of Africa. And together we turned our eyes to the small light-space, and our sadness grew. When the guard called me to leave, I would kiss Saa's head gently and bow my head into her sweet fur.

Soon, Saa. Soon. But I don't know how.

Chapter Eight

Today the High Lord sent for me. One of the low-women came to me with no smile on her face and a dress over her shoulder.

She flung the dress at me. 'You are to wear this,' she said roughly. 'And hurry.'

But it was hard to hurry when my fingers were trembling so that I couldn't fasten the buttons of the linen dress.

We went up through the decks, travelling in a cage made of glass that they have, so that even as you shiver from the chill of the cool-vents, you can see the hot, brown land and imagine being free.

'In there,' she said, pushing me towards a door painted black with a silver handle. She turned quickly and was gone, back to wherever she came from. Did she have a daughter? I wondered.

Did she have a heart, as my mother had? Or was she just there to serve and eat and sleep until the days passed, and her time here was over?

'Come,' said a deep voice, when I knocked. I went in.

It was Sharon's grandfather.

He didn't smile or say anything. He just looked at me. I tried to keep my eyes lowered respectfully, but I wanted to look at him too. I wanted to see these people who ran this island and had taken my lion and my life.

'Have you seen enough?' he said sharply, after a moment. I looked down.

'I'm sorry,' I whispered.

'It is *I* who wish to see *you*,' he added, less sharply. And he was staring at me hard, as if he would imprint my face on his memory for ever.

'You are the granddaughter of Habbi Rava?' he asked.

Grandmother's name! My heart thudded in my chest.

'Yes.'

'Speak up!'

'Yes!'

'A troublesome woman,' he said, unsmiling. 'Very troublesome.'

But the mention of her name – a name that everyone knew, but nobody called her by, had quietened my heart and focused my mind. How did this ... this Lord ... this king of the island, know of her? What did he know of her? And, most important, what would grandmother do if she were here? How would she use this opportunity to her advantage ... to the advantage of all of us?

And then her voice seemed to sound softly in my ear, and I listened to her words again:

'Rain! You must stay sharp and aware. You must listen with every part of yourself and watch, and scent, and taste. You must find out everything that there is to find.'

So I did.

I looked at the carpet. It was a gentle blue, like the sky on a winter day. Where my toes curled over the edge of my sandals, it was soft. The things in the room were of no use to me. But my feelings were.

The High Lord was talking about The Island. As I looked down at the blue, I listened to the heart behind the words and I knew that he was angry – angry and afraid.

'Nothing will harm this island, or my people!' he was saying. 'Not while I draw breath!'

He glared at me furiously, as if I was the threat

he dreaded. 'Tell me...' he said – and I thought he was making an effort to be calm, to control his temper – 'tell me about these *ceremonies* you have.'

I looked up at him then, making my eyes puzzled and uncertain. 'Ceremonies?'

'Yes,' he snarled. 'These ceremonies with lions that you do.'

It was not hard to look afraid. It was much harder to look lost and stupid – but he must have thought I was, because suddenly he turned, sweeping his long linen robe out of the way impatiently. Then he turned back and looked at me closely.

I tried to empty my mind of Grandmother and the lion-pictures on the walls of the caves. I tried to forget her words of wisdom. I forgot, as hard as I could, the sound of her voice, the touch of her strong, brown hand. In my mind she no longer existed, because the High Lord was looking there for her – and I was determined that he was *not* going to find her.

I tried to seem stupid. I thought about the time I had climbed up to get honey, forgetting about the sting of bees. I remembered the sharp little pains of their anger and how I had fallen to the ground, winded and crying. And how there had been no sympathy from grandmother and no soothing herbs for my stings and cuts and grazes. 'Stupid!' she had said, when I ran to her later. 'Stupid.'

So that's what I was. And I remembered so well her disappointment and her contempt... that I felt slow tears creep out of my eyes and run down my cheeks, dripping off my chin on to the blue carpet that was like the sky on a winter's day. And I cried even more because I had abandoned a person that I loved, and I closed her from my heart. I was lost.

The High Lord made an angry sound, and I knew my plan had worked, because he spoke only to himself, under his breath. 'Stupid!' he said. 'Stupid!' And then he smiled, for the first time. 'You must have been a great disappointment to her,' he said in a pleased voice.

Then it was I who was angry. Hot light fired through my heart and my blood. But I looked down and snivelled some more.

'Go,' he said, turning away in disgust. 'I have no use for you!'

It took some time to find my way back to the lower decks of the city. Nobody was around. Everything was quiet, It was afternoon rest time. I crept, like a little mouse, down flights of steps and along narrow corridors, until at last I came to a place I remembered, and knew where to find Saa.

The guard was not pleased to see me. 'You are late!' he said crossly. He jerked his thumb in the direction of Saa's cage. 'She's not happy.'

My heart almost stopped when I saw her. Saa was completely still. Not even the end of her tail twitched when I called her name. The guard grumpily opened her cage. Normally he was cautious, but today he didn't care. He seemed more interested in his lunch, as if ... as if she was dead.

After he closed the door, I lay down beside Saa, the whole length of my body pressed against her. She was still breathing, but in small, short breaths, as if she were too tired to care about air, and her heartbeat was slow and still.

For a moment I laid my head down on hers. The tears still ran down my cheeks. Now that I had remembered Grandmother and the bees, now that I had made it so real, it was in my heart: I was a failure. A failure and a disappointment, as the High Lord had said. And she had gone, gone from me. I had forced her out of my heart. I was alone.

We lay together, Saa and I, still and sad, and the time ticked past like the clock in the great hall that measures the passing of the day for the Tekkies. *Click, click ... click, click...* The time was running out of my life, my life and Saa's.

And then, very slowly, Saa licked my hand. Her tongue was rough like sand under my feet. It hurt a bit, but I didn't notice. It was as if all the pain in my world was concentrated on that small part of me where my lion loved me.

For a moment more I lay still. I had been to a place where I never wished to be again – a dead place where there was no hope, no love. And Saa had brought me back.

I sat up and rubbed my face clean on the stupid dress. Then I took Saa's great head in my hands, so that her eyelids fluttered and she half-opened her golden eyes.

'Saa! I am going to find help. I am going to get you out of here. I am going to get you home. And we are *not* giving up!'

Chapter Nine

The guard let me out without comment. He didn't care. He watched me pass him in the narrow tunnel and then locked the door after me. I heard him yawning as he settled down in his chair near the door. It was boring and hot down here.

I had no idea what to do. I had to get help – urgent help – for Saa. But who would care? Who would know anything about lions?

As I hurried back above deck, I was thinking about Ghau. He lived a secret life here on the island, coming and going as he pleased. There was no talk of him among the low-people (who knew everything that went on here) and no snide questions from Sharon (who thought she did). It was as if he was invisible. So how was I going to find him?

'Looking for something?'

It was Sharon. She stood blocking my way, with the sun behind her. I had to raise my hand to shield my eyes against the glare.

She was looking at me closely – the linen dress, the dirt I had collected and the grass in my hair from holding Saa, the tear-stains on my face.

'So…?' she said.

I couldn't see her face properly, but I knew her one golden eyebrow would be raised in that way she had, a way she had copied from a V-Disk story we had once seen.

And then it struck me. Sharon had no business to be down here! Was she trying to find Saa on her own?

'Yes,' I said quickly. 'I was looking for you. I've just remembered. There was a message – from Nam – for you. I forgot to give it to you. I'm sorry.' I hung my head as if ashamed.

Inside, I was wondering how I had learned to lie so easily.

'He said … Nam said … for you to meet him at the Stravanga Dome, now.' I had no idea what time it was, but I took a guess. 'At three.' The words came out in a big rush, as if I had practised them.

Sharon looked at me for a moment. Nam had never spoken to me before, let alone asked me to pass messages. She was suspicious – but this was something she wanted to believe. So she did.

'Well, next time, make sure you deliver!' she snapped. She looked at the clock they all wear on their wrists to remind them when to connect and disconnect from the enhancers and recharge their ion extractors, and when to report for activities. It must have been close to the time I had said.

She gave me an angry look and turned away. I heard her heels tapping on the metal floor. 'I'll talk to you about this later!' she called over her shoulder.

I leaned against the metal wall of the corridor. It was burning hot. My knees were trembling. Everything was happening too fast.

Where was I going to get medicine for Saa? In my homeland there were plants – roots and berries and sweet, green, growing things. Grandmother knew about them, and she had taught me a little. I would go to her and she would tell me what to search for, and I would bring the things to her and she would make a powder, or an ointment, or a mixture with river water, and I would give it to Saa – as I had done when she had hurt her paw once on the sharp stones of the cave-cliff.

Here there was a clinic. Sharon went there sometimes for headache pills. I knew where it was, but what would I do when I got there? My hand slipped to my waist, where I wore my small, sharp knife under my clothes. I could, maybe, creep up behind the clinic person and make them give me something. Medicine that was good for Tekkies must be good for lions – if you gave them more of it.

It wasn't a good plan, but it was the only one I could think of. I began to run.

It turned out to be a very bad plan.

When I got there, the clinic door was open and a Tekkie in a white dress was talking to someone I couldn't see.

'...Not what I've been used to ... all these shortages ... and no new equipment for the last two years. It's getting serious, I tell you ... serious... And the Stats ... well, everyone knows what the Stats are telling us... If we don't get some rain soon – somewhere – there's going to be trouble... *Big* trouble...'

The other person mumbled something and the Tekkie laughed.

'No, I don't think the Lords have got a clue! My husband says – and I agree with him...'

Her voice dropped to a more discreet level, and I couldn't hear any more.

My plan of sneaking in with my small sharp knife and holding it to her throat until she gave me lion medicine began to seem childish. She might have been a Tekkie, but still, she was a human being with real blood in her ... and a husband who disapproved of the Lords ... and who knows how many children. This wasn't a V-Disk. This was real. My knees were trembling. I gripped the knife tighter... Maybe I could *make* myself do this, for Saa.

It was then that a hand was clamped over my mouth, a knee pressed hard against my back, and everything went dark...

I thought I was back ... back on the journey, back in time and place ... back at the beginning. But there was no camel movement this time, just strong arms that roughly swept me off my feet and into the darkness of a sack. And then I was being carried, and there were quiet, urgent voices that I strained to hear through the thick cloth.

And then there was Ghau, and he was holding my hand and saying my name and calling someone a fool. And somebody gave me a sip of water and I spat out the foul taste of the sack and wondered what had happened to me.

'It's time,' Ghau said, and I saw the excitement in his eyes. 'There are people … there are Mainlanders from Out. They are ready to take us! Now! Today!'

And when I didn't say anything, because my mind was too full of Saa, he went on: 'And you nearly ruined it. What were you doing down there with your knife in your hand, all ready to spring? Like a little lion?' He looked at me fondly, as if I had done something foolish, but nothing he couldn't sort out for me.

'Saa, ' I said. 'Saa … I think she is going to die. I went to get medicine for her.' The words were like a knife in my heart, as if saying them would harm her more.

The excitement and joy faded. 'What! But we must leave now – this instant! This man,' and he nodded towards the man who stood guard beside the door, 'has come to take us. There is a way, a secret way to a place where we can get out. They have a boat – but it must be now!'

Ghau looked around him, as if someone would appear to confirm what he was saying. But there was nobody except the hooded figure, and he kept his head down, saying nothing.

I shook my head. 'Saa cannot lift her head. She cannot walk. And I will never go without her. Never.'

Ghau looked at me. It was a look I can never forget because it said so much. I was hurting him. He measured me with his eyes and he was disappointed in what he saw.

'But, Rain...' And then he turned away. I went on looking at the place where his eyes had been.

After a moment he spoke, and his voice was flat and still like the sea before a storm.

'She will not go,' he said to the man, and his voice faltered. 'I know her … a little … and I know this: Rain will not leave without the lion. Never.' He looked desperate. 'The lion is too heavy for us to move. It can't be done.'

I reached out and touched Ghau's arm, and his look flickered back to mine. I thought what it would mean for him to be away from this terrible place, back on the land he loved. But chief in my mind was Saa, and the still place which was all that was left of my once-lion. My heart would break in two if I had to leave her.

As Ghau turned away, I grabbed at him and he turned back, but the blaze had gone from him and he could not look at me.

'But *you* must go!' I said. 'You must go without me.'

He shook his head. 'No. You don't understand.' He spoke sadly. He bowed his head. His voice was so low that I could barely hear what he said.

'You don't understand. You will never leave Saa – but I … I can never leave *you*.'

Chapter Ten

What had I done? What had I done to Ghau?

The hooded man left, seeing that there was no persuading me. His boat waited for the turn of the tide, waited on the dangerous rocks where Ghau and Saa and I should now have been, waiting for nightfall and safety and freedom. I could not bear to think of it.

Ghau took me back to my deck and promised to return with medicines for Saa. And of course he did. But he stopped me when I tried to thank him. 'The Writer got hold of them,' he said shortly. 'He still has some herbs and powders from his old life, from before. He says they are very strong. She should be better in a few days.' And in his voice was the regret that I felt too, and longing for the sound of the clean wind across the living land and the green places. When I tried to speak, he stopped me, saying he must hurry, he had things to do.

When he left, he took with him the little hope I had begun to feel.

I made the guard get milk for Saa, and eggs. He brought them reluctantly. I thought I saw a look of fear in his expression when I told him what he must do, as if he was afraid of me. I stirred the powders The Writer had sent into the mixture and fed it to Saa, drop by drop, as often as she would take it.

I was excused other duties – they wanted their lion alive, apparently.

Sharon didn't give me much trouble when I mumbled that maybe I had got things mixed up, that maybe it wasn't Nam who had given me the message. Sharon didn't care. She had confronted Nam when he didn't arrive at the meeting place and although he denied all knowledge of the message, it had given him the opportunity to ask her to go to see a V-Disk with him. That was all Sharon wanted. She didn't care about me, and she seemed to have given up wanting to see Lion, now that she had Nam to think about. She didn't even ask about the dress, and the tears.

So my days passed with Saa. Slowly, her strength

began to return to her. But I worried about her. Her life-force seemed small, thin … faded. She still looked towards the light in her cage, but hopelessly, as if she did not expect ever to feel again the joy of running free and the thrill of the hunt. I grieved for her. I grieved for Ghau. And a small part of me grieved for me – for Rain. What would become of us all?

Now, because we had glimpsed freedom, The Island became impossible to bear. Wherever I looked there were hard walls, hard voices, hard faces. I kept quiet, kept my head down, spent as much time as I could with Saa.

And still I talked to her. There was nobody there to care except her, nobody to hear except her. I told her of the time when I had been very young and there had been a great dance and people had gathered from all the villages. The old people had sat together, telling stories about the old days and laughing, laughing. That was the sound I longed to hear: laughter.

'…And Saa, people lit a great fire to cook a goat – one you didn't get that time, Saa! And they shared out the meat, leaving nobody out – even the smallest children and the old people who didn't have many teeth – somebody cut it up for them.

And Ala told a story about the hunter who was hunted by the porcupine, and got a hundred quills stuck in his behind that his wife had to take out for him when he got home. And, oh, how they laughed – and the hunter laughed most of all!

'And there was the time we went collecting food from the bush, and there was a snake in the tree, and the boys laughed because we were talking so much that we didn't even see it – and they chased it away with sticks.

'And I remember the night of my little brother's feast, the night when he stopped being a child and went into the bush to learn to be a man. Oh, Saa, how I remember that night, and how we danced to the moon, and the dust rose under our feet in little clouds and the stars shone brightly. Stars like tears, shining in the sky.'

And then my voice seemed to run away somewhere and stop, and I could not go on. 'And then they stole us.'

Ghau had arrived so silently that I had not known he was there.

'Rain...' he said, and my heart turned over. 'Rain, I came to tell you...'

He squatted down beside me. 'I hate to hear you sound so unhappy.'

I tried to laugh. 'Is that what you came to tell me?'

'No,' he said. 'I came to say I am sorry. I didn't understand ... I *don't* understand ... about Saa. I should have thought more. I'm sorry.'

But it was I who was sorry. I took a deep breath. The words I would speak now were important words, maybe the most important words I would ever speak.

'Ghau, you are ... you are my friend ... my best of friends, my only friend.' I looked straight at him, his dark, almond eyes unwavering.

'But Saa...' I went on, 'you must understand, she's not a pet! She is my life. She is what I was born to do!' I could hear the desperation in my voice. I had missed Ghau so much during these last weeks. 'I don't understand! I don't know things like you – like The Writer. I know nothing – except that Saa is my duty, my responsibility...'

'And your love,' Ghau finished for me.

'And my love.' I looked at him directly. 'And my love. But that doesn't mean that there can be no other love in my heart' – I whispered the last words – 'for you.'

We were quiet. Ghau didn't speak. I couldn't speak.

'Thank you,' he said at last. 'I will hold those words close.'

Then we spoke of other things, but I felt the lightness come back to me, and the hope.

Chapter Eleven

Something is happening. There is a sense of urgency, of change, the thrill of danger in the air, like the idea of rain before the clouds come.

Today there was a ceremony. The Tekkies have had them before, gathering according to age group in the Pleasure Dome where the Stravangas are held, covering their heads with fine shawls out of respect. I have seen them coming and going to such meetings while I have been busy about my work, but this time low-people were ordered to attend as well. This was unusual.

Sharon was there, of course, but she was not interested in me. Nam was standing at the front of the Dome, so that's where she wriggled herself through the crowd. He pretended not to notice her at first, but I could see from where I was standing that he had seen her, and at last he half-turned and nodded to her. She looked ridiculously happy when he did.

Then a small bell rang (no sirens for now) and the five Lords came in. They too wore their shawls of respect and they stood for a moment, heads bowed, waiting for complete quiet.

Sharon's grandfather was there. She turned round and gave me a smug look when she saw him, just to remind me, I suppose, of how well-connected she was.

But, when silence came and the Lords raised their heads, I nearly fell to the ground with shock. Last in line, looking straight at me, was The Writer!

I heard nothing of what was said in that first few minutes. He held my eyes with his, strong and powerful, as if willing me not to react. And indeed, I could not have. My mind was choked with thoughts, questions, ideas. I kept very still and did not drop my gaze.

After a time, he half-smiled and turned away. He was pleased, but I didn't know why. What did it mean?

When my mind returned to where I was, they were talking about a great ceremony that was to be held. Another Stravanga? No, not this time.

This was to be something extraordinary.

'There have been signs,' the Head Lord was saying. 'For twenty years we have seen signs of change, and now we can predict with certainty that change is happening.' Then he said a lot about the Book of Stats that they all follow so anxiously, and how the rain patterns have shown signs of changing and the temperature lines are doing something else.

I didn't understand the words, but a picture came into my mind of my own sweet river flowing bravely across the desert. I wondered if change was coming there, too.

'It has been decided,' he went on loudly – and his voice battered at my ears like the endless waves below – 'that there will be a Grand Ceremony.'

A little gasp ... a flutter ... an intake of breath from the assembled young Tekkies. His eyes snapped over them and they were still.

'Some of you will be too young to have experienced such a ceremony before. It is,' he reminded them, 'a most solemn thing. There will be study, and fasting, and thought.'

A glance passed between Nam and Sharon. They were not pleased by this.

There were more instructions, more orders

and procedures. Servant-people were to report to their Deck-keepers for further instructions. All Stravangas were cancelled until after the Grand Ceremony. Respect shawls were to be worn at all times until further notice. Life, for the Tekkies, was not going to be easy.

When the High Lord had finished, the age groups streamed out of the Dome. They seemed quiet enough but inside, I sensed, they were bristling with indignation.

I was not surprised when Ghau summoned me late that evening. I had been asleep in the worker cell that I share with three other girls, deeply asleep after a long hot day. Suddenly I was awake.

'You must come,' he whispered, his words soft as a stir of air on a still afternoon. 'It is time.'

Time? My heart leapt.

And this time I was ready. Saa was ready. We could go, leave, shake off the dust of this evil place.

Ghau took me to a small, rich room on the High Deck where I had been taken to see the High Lord. Wearing respect shawls to disguise ourselves, we slipped along quiet corridors, until at last Ghau knocked on a green wooden door.

The Writer's voice called that we should enter.

It was a room unlike anything I had expected.

It was… soft. The Writer saw my surprise.

'One becomes accustomed to all this,' he said. 'This is the way we Lords live.'

Then he surprised me by laughing, and he asked me: 'When have you been happiest in your life?'

My mind flickered. Images passed behind my eyes: laughing with my mother and the other women on the night of my brother's coming-of-age. Water-drops sparkling in sunlight on my river. Ghau's gentle touch, the day he came to see Saa. Saa…

'The night when Saa first came home to me,' I said, raising my look to his. 'That is when I was happiest. When she and I became Lion.' I could see that my answer had pleased The Writer. Ghau didn't react. Maybe he understood.

'You must be ready,' The Writer said. 'Soon you will leave this place. You are going home. You are taking Saa home. Is she ready? Are *you* ready?' Again that little half-smile, as if he was remembering the last time he had tried to help us leave.

'We are ready,' I said firmly. Now he had stopped smiling and was serious again. 'This time there must be no mistake. There won't be another opportunity. The tides are right. The moon is dark … and we are running out of time. This is our last chance.'

'But, before you leave, I want you to understand some things ... about Tekkies... about the change that is coming ... about yourself.'

I nodded. Maybe at last I was to have answers to my questions.

He glanced over his shoulder, as if someone could be listening, but Ghau nodded. 'It is safe – for now,' he said quietly, and The Writer went on.

'I have heard,' he said, 'that you are bothered by the question of betrayal – of who told the Tekkies about you.'

I nodded again. Had Ghau told him?

He leaned forward. 'You must understand,' he said, 'that the Tekkies are not the only ones who can send messages and listen to words. *Our* people – our old people – have always known the stories of the land. And you are part of that story. You were known about when you were born, and spoken of wherever people talked of such things around their fires on quiet nights. You are Habbi Rava's granddaughter. You are the Keeper of Lion.'

He paused.

'You must not underestimate your own people. They do not have the shiny things that the Tekkies have.' He looked angry again, and then he seemed to control his thoughts, and went on: 'But our people have knowledge and understanding. We care about each other. We can bring back to this Earth what we have lost as people, as humans. And you, and Ghau, and Saa are to be part of that. This has been spoken of. Our Elder People have spoken of it. Your grandmother and I spoke of it when we met ten moons ago.'

He smiled at my look of surprise. 'I told you, do not underestimate us!'

Then he stopped smiling.

'And yes, the Tekkies knew about you too. They have always known.'

I felt a little shiver of fear.

'They were waiting until you were ready, but you were not ready when their need was greatest, so they took you anyway.

'They sent their messengers, the Travellers – traders who are everywhere over the land of Africa, bringing things, selling things ... taking things. They sent such men to find you and seize you and Saa and bring you here. They did not know what they would do with you. They expected, I think, for you to somehow tell them. But you have not!"

I felt a small warmth of approval. I had not told them anything! And then I remembered how little I knew that would be of use to them.

But The Writer seemed to understand.

'You have puzzled them,' he said quietly. 'They do not understand you because you appear so young, so weak – and yet so strong. They don't understand how you do that. They have watched you and you have not wavered, have not broken. They are afraid of you.'

A small noise distracted him, and Ghau moved quickly to the door – then nodded. The Writer went on, speaking faster now.

'Change is always with us,' he said. 'Change happens in every part of every smallest part of time. You may think that this time, for you, will never end. But it will.' He leaned forward, suddenly fierce; '*It will!*'

'There is a point where change becomes something that cannot be stopped. A small matter, perhaps, of one raindrop more that makes the stream begin to flow. And when that happens, it cannot be reversed. That is about to happen – to you, to us, to our world.'

He looked at me encouragingly. 'But where there is change, there is always – *always* – fear. That is something you must be aware of. The Tekkies know that change is coming. They have their measurements that tell them so, their holy book of statistics and notifications and numbers. So they are afraid. And when people are afraid, they are dangerous. Very dangerous.

'The Tekkies have always been afraid, since first their world began to crumble and change. And instead of changing with it, they have retreated, trying to make things stay the same as they once were.' He shook his head. 'That cannot be done. It is impossible.

'Now change is coming faster than they can defend themselves against it. They are even more afraid – and even more dangerous. You will have to be very strong, and very careful.'

Part of me wanted to hide away where nobody could find me. Part of me was like a small, weak creature with no will to fight. Part of me wanted my mother to hold me close. Part of me wanted to run away. But what, then, would happen to Saa?

'I am ready,' I told The Writer. He held my eyes for a moment, then looked away. 'There is little I can give you,' he said at last, 'that can help you. Except, perhaps this...' He placed a small leather bag, heavy in my outstretched hand. I put it safe in my buttoned pocket alongside with my knife. 'This may help in places where gold has some meaning. Keep it close. I have supplies for Ghau to take, ready for the journey you must make. And…'

He stopped. Ghau was gently tugging my arm. There were voices approaching, arguing voices, angry voices. It was time to go.

We slipped, silent as mice, through a small door that led into another corridor, one used, perhaps, by servants. The door closed behind us with a tiny click and we leaned against the wall, silent, listening.

'It is time, I tell you!' one voice said coldly. It was the Head Lord. 'We can wait no longer. Bring the Grand Ceremony forward.'

The Writer's voice was calm. 'It is too soon,' he said. 'The people are not prepared. There must be fasting … there must be respect…'

'No.' It was another of the Lords speaking. 'No. The time for delay is over. It must be tomorrow. The sacrifice must be tomorrow. That is my decision.'

My heart turned icy. Sacrifice? My mind leaped to Saa. Were they going to sacrifice Saa?

Then there were running feet and more voices shouting, and the world seemed to tilt under my feet.

'The lion! The lion has gone!'

Chapter Twelve

Everything went dark, black, cold.

I felt Ghau's arms round me, holding me up, and his voice soft against my ear, murmuring my name. 'Rain … oh, Rain. You must be strong. You must be strong … for Saa, and for me.'

And my mind came back from the place it had flown to, fluttering and limp like a dying bird, and I leaned against Ghau and took from his warmth and strength.

The voices were raised again inside the rich room. I could hear The Writer's steady voice pleading for calm, then the Lords' voices, angry and harsh. I remembered that they were afraid – and I could hear it in their voices.

'What are we going to do?' I whispered.

Ghau took my hand and we slipped silently

along the corridor, through a small opening I would never have seen but he knew of, and down, down into the tunnels and walkways of the underside of The Island. I touched my knife for reassurance. Yes, I would use it if I had to.

We knew Saa wasn't there, but we went anyway to the place where she had been imprisoned. The air hung empty with the scent of her and a drying paw-print on the metal floor was fading, but just visible, where her water bowl had spilt. The guard snored in his usual place with his mouth open, an empty bottle in his hand. What had happened here? His relief guard must have come to change shifts and raised the alarm.

Ghau pointed to the print. 'She can't have gone far,' he said. 'They must have raised the alarm immediately. We have time.'

My mind had stopped thinking about anything except Saa. When I cracked my elbow against a pipe as we ran, I felt no pain, although I noticed briefly that there was blood. My feet moved of their own will, swiftly following where Ghau led. I felt nothing. I was strong. I could do anything – would do anything – to find Saa.

Ghau paused at a place where two tunnels divided, one narrower, dusty. There were few lights this far down, but he crouched low under the faint orange glow from one. He looked puzzled.

'Saa came here,' he said. 'But there are traces of people here in the dust, people running. Tekkies.'

I leaned against the wall, getting my breath back; trying to clear my brain and think.

'But Tekkies don't come down here.'

'These two did.'

We looked at each other, and that look was enough to tell us that we were both thinking the same thing. We set off again, running swiftly now, Ghau reading the signs of the lion and the fleeing people.

We found them at the next intersection of the tunnels. We were far below decks now and it was hot, even though it was night up above. No cool air reached down here and the air pumps strained against the heat.

'Rain! Rain!' Sharon screamed at me. 'Help us!'

She was wedged high up among the pipes and wires and tubes that ran the length of the tunnels. Her face was bone-white, smeared with dirt, and her eyes huge and terrified.

Saa was crouched almost flat against the tunnel floor, a low, angry sound in her throat. Her eyes flashed green fire. At her feet lay the body of a boy – Nam. She was gathering herself to spring and she paused, uncertain what to do, which way to attack.

'We only went to have a look!' Sharon whimpered. 'We didn't mean to let it out... Nam said he'd seen a V-Disk about lion-training. He said it would be fun! I ... I didn't know how strong it would be – how fast.'

Across my memory flashed her earlier words: *I've never seen a wild animal.* They were Tekkies. How could they know what power – what anger and hurt – lay coiled in that great cat, waiting?

Saa was confused. I could see that. Ghau stood frozen at my side. He knew what Lion can do.

Softly I called her name, gentling her with my voice. 'Saa, my lion, my child. You must stop this now. You must come with me where we will be safe. I've come to get you.'

Saa looked back at Nam, sprawled awkwardly in front of her. Was he dead? Had she killed him?

And then my Saa, my friend and my lion, stood up, and in that standing she brought back to herself all her grace and strength and power. And she yawned once, long and huge, opening her great muzzle so that Sharon shrieked again at the rows of shining teeth. She curled her tongue back delicately and looked straight into my eyes.

For a long moment she stared. I felt that she was seeing into my soul. She stepped slowly towards me until she stood at my side, and my trembling fingers found the rough fur of her head, and we were still.

At once Ghau was at Nam's side, his fingers finding the pulse in the boy's neck.

'He's alive,' he said briefly. My heart fluttered.

Ghau swiftly checked him over, lifting his limbs gently, searching for blood. 'Something else did this. Not Saa.'

'He … he hit his head when he tried to jump up,' Sharon said shakily. 'He put me up here first, but when he jumped himself, he cracked his head. It was awful. That monster could have killed him.'

Ghau straightened up, ignoring Sharon and looking at me. 'Is this the one you told me about?'

I nodded.

'And she says she knows the way to the beach? The way to Out?'

'Yes.'

He turned to Sharon. 'Do you?' he asked.

Sharon seemed to be getting some of her old spirit back now that Nam was safe. 'Well, what if I do?' she said, tossing her hair back.

'Then you can take Rain and Saa to the place you know of, right now, before the guards find us.'

With some difficulty, Sharon climbed down from her perch. Neither of us helped her. Then she was on the floor again, dusty but defiant.

'I never meant to take Rain there, anyway!' she sneered. 'It was just a trick to see the creature. Nam and I did it on our own, without any help from her. All it took was a bottle of spirit for that stupid guard!'

Ghau's voice was steady. 'And without her help,' he said mildly, 'your friend here would be dead and you might be too. Lions can jump up, you know.'

Sharon didn't look grateful. 'Well, I'm not going to take her!'

Ghau looked carefully at the knife that had been ready in his hand all this time.

'I have a knife. Rain has a knife. Rain also has a lion.' He looked at her and his eyes blazed. 'Now, take her to the beach!'

Sharon shot me a look of pure hatred. Whatever she did, she was already in deep trouble. The Lords would not easily forgive her for this... But even worse was the fact that she had let Saa escape – let their sacrifice go.

'Rain' – Ghau's hand was on my wrist again – 'you must go with her to the way out. I think she does know where it is. And you know what to do if she doesn't.'

'Yes.'

'I will follow, but first I must go back. I will track you there.'

I knew now that he could. Ghau could read the tunnels as others read a map. But why did he have to go back?

Briefly he leaned towards me, his breath warm against my face. 'Be careful! Be careful of her words.' Then he slipped back into the shadows and was gone.

I made Sharon walk ahead with Saa behind her and me following. I reminded her of the strength of Lion. I told her that Saa had not eaten live kill for many moons. I thought I would frighten her, but Sharon wasn't frightened easily.

She paused, uncertain, but then she led us into a tunnel that led down, so far down that we began to hear the dull thud and roar of the water. The air was fresher, cooler, and there was the clean smell of salt.

And then she began to talk. Softly, without raising her voice, but her words were poisoning the new air, and my heart.

'You won't get far,' she said confidently. 'I'll take you to a door that leads to Out – oh, I do know where there is one – an old service entrance that isn't used now – and I'll tell them you made me take you … with that … that *thing*. I'll tell them you forced me with a knife to let it loose, and made Nam and me help you escape.'

She turned in the dusty passage to smile at me, her confidence returning with every lie she invented. 'And I'll tell them about that boy – whoever he is – and they will scour this rock from top to bottom, and then all of you will die! They can have a really good sacrifice! Not just you, but that … *thing* … and the boy too.'

I felt faint. 'What are you talking about?'

She stopped and turned round, so that she could watch my face. 'Didn't you know? The Grand Ceremony tomorrow … it's for you. It's going to be a sacrifice, and it's *you* they are going to kill!'

She thought that telling me this would be the worst thing she could say to me. But it wasn't – because it was not what I was expecting her to say.

Then my heart hardened against Sharon. She was not, nor ever had been, my friend.

I didn't let her talk any more. When she objected, I pushed the knife against her and pricked her skin so that she yelped in fear. 'I have nothing to lose by killing you,' I said. 'Nothing. Now, shut up and walk.' I hope my voice sounded brave. I didn't feel brave. I wished Ghau would come.

Down and down we went, nearer and nearer to the sea. Then, far below us were lights, and guards – and far behind us the sound of sirens and alarms. The Lords had finally decided to make public the fact that their sacrifice was escaping.

Chapter Thirteen

We walked in silence now. Sharon seemed to have given up, but I didn't trust her. The sound of the sea was beating against my brain. The dusty tunnel grew smaller, more cramped, but the air was fresher, almost chill, and there was the scent of salt.

And then suddenly the tunnel ended. We all stopped.

'I said I'd bring you,' Sharon said, 'and I have. I never said you could go out, though!' Her voice rang with triumph and spite.

I saw that the way ahead was barred. Wooden boards had been nailed roughly over the entrance. Maybe, once, stores had been loaded here, but now the way was closed and on the other side there was nothing. No steps. No ladder. No way to climb down.

Through the cracks I could see pale stars – there was no moon tonight – and the faint shape of the land far, far below, on the other side of the waves. There was no escape here.

And behind us the clamour of sirens grew and swelled, roaring like waves of anger, getting closer. Caught between Sharon's shrill voice and the scream of the sirens, there was no space in my head to think.

But Sharon had forgotten the power of Lion.

Saa raised her great head at the scent of freedom, the scent of the sweet, sweet land and of space and stars. She crouched, her tail swishing angrily at the sound of Sharon's voice, her powerful hindquarters tensed and ready.

And then she jumped.

The rotten boards splintered at the weight and power of her and, even as I cried her name, she crashed through into empty space. Gone. I heard my scream follow her, down and down until it, too, disappeared into the black hold of the night and the sea.

There was a roaring in my ears. Saa, my life, my friend and my heart…

Sharon smiled her cat-smile.

'Give up?' she asked, sweetly.

No! I would not give up!

I did not pause to think. Without a further thought, I threw myself out through the gap after Saa, floating free... down, down towards the white of the waves and the black of the rock, calling, calling, calling her name: *Saaaaaaaaaaaaaaaaaa...*

᠅

The chill of the water was shocking, when I hit it. But the pain in my heart was worse than any physical pain. My Saa was gone. It did not matter if I lived or died.

But I *did* live.

I swam.

The noise of the sea, the distant sirens from The Island, faded away. The Island was a dream. Only the cold, cold water was real, the sound of water moving, sweeping, roaring in my ears.

Then I thought I could hear the laughter of children and the calls of mothers with their babies in the brown, sun-splashed water of my own sweet river, my own place. I lay for a moment on the water, as my brother had taught me in our silk-smooth river, and the salt brine held me gently for a heartbeat, and there was peace. Then, in my dream,

I was with Saa and she had come to the moonlit river with me, to drink and to lie in the cool water after the heat of the day, to play.

And then the sea had me again in its teeth. Currents pulled me. I had no sense of direction, I could barely keep myself afloat in the salt of the sea, gasping and choking on it, holding on to my dream.

And then I dreamed of my mother, and my grandmother, and they were smiling and holding out their arms to me in welcome, and I was home at last. And there was Ghau, smiling too, waiting for me.

I stopped swimming.

Chapter Fourteen

I was dead. I knew that, because Saa was there, and Ghau, and I knew that my mother and my grandmother were somewhere close. My fingers touched Saa's fur, warm from the sunlight of home. She breathed beneath my touch. Maybe I was in heaven...

Somebody was giving me small sips of a liquid that was cool and sweet and tasted of berries from Wild. And Ghau was saying my name in a way that I would never have dared to dream, over and over again, softly like the music of stars: 'Rain. Rain. Rain.'

And then I was not dead, but cold and aching in every bone in my body and trying to sit up, and there was a roaring in my ears that deafened out even the waves.

'Saa … where is she? Where's Saa?'

'Oh, Rain,' Ghau breathed. 'You have come back to me! And Saa is safe, but only just. I found her first and carried you back to her.' He laughed softly, and I could feel the laughter in the trembling of his chest as he held me. 'It was easier than carrying her to you. And I thought the two of you had better be together!'

And slowly I came back from the dream and saw that I was lying on the cool sand of Out. I was with Ghau and he was happy. So I was too.

Saa was lying deep in the shadow of some huge rocks. As soon as I could stand, Ghau helped me over to her. She was lying very still, but her breath came warm and steady when I put my face beside hers.

'She nearly drowned, I think,' Ghau said softly. 'But she was thrown out by the waves and must have crawled up here.' He did not say it, but I guessed that she must have been near death, here on this beach so far away from home … without me.

I stroked Saa's damp fur.

'She's resting. Her strength will come back. Don't be afraid, Rain. She will run with you again in the valleys of Mpopo and the sun will shine for you.'

My eyes closed. I could not keep them open. I laid down my head, and it was held close and true and warm, and Ghau was with me in a place where we would always be safe. It was the sweetest sleep I had ever known.

After a time I woke. It was cold. Ghau was still there. Saa slept still.

Then I saw a strange light coming from The Island. Hungry flames licked along the decks and there were puffs of heat and smoke from every side.

I turned my head and Ghau murmured my name.

'What happened?'

'The Writer,' Ghau said briefly, and a shadow passed over his face. 'He was ready … but everything moved too fast for him. There was not enough time for him to finish his plans for us.'

I looked at The Island and even as I watched, a great explosion beat against the air, sending even mightier flames up towards the stars in sheets of fire and showers of sparks.

'The Writer … is he …?'

Ghau sighed deeply. 'He could not escape. It all happened too quickly. First there were the alarms, and guards were summoned. Then they announced the sacrifice...' His voice trembled.

'But the sacrifice had escaped. Everybody on that rock was mobilised to find you. It was only a matter of time before they did. And we were not to know which opening Sharon would take you to – or that you would jump. Nobody thought you would escape. No one has ever escaped.'

We were quiet for a moment. I remembered Saa's great leap against the splintering wood and my cry as I followed. As for Ghau... I don't know what he was thinking, but his arms tightened around me.

'I went back for the supplies The Writer had ready for us – and for his final instructions.' Ghau nodded towards a pack that lay behind my head. 'And then I followed your trail. The Writer covered my back. He knew of a power control that would damage the machinery of The Island. He went back there when we said goodbye ... alone. It was the only chance he could give us.'

We were silent.

I thought about the Tekkies and this island place where they had tried to hide away. I thought of the life they had built for themselves behind the great metal plates and the way they had clung to their old ways. I thought about the woman in the clinic with the husband who didn't think much of the Lords. I thought about Sharon. I thought about The Writer... and tears crept down my cheeks and dripped on to the sand, silently. I hadn't said goodbye to The Writer.

'Don't,' Ghau said. 'Don't think back. We have to go on now.'

He stood, stretching his arms above his head stiffly. 'There are men coming. Men from Out who are desperate for change. The Writer found them. They will take us into Drylands – they have some fossil fuel they have hoarded. They will take us as far as they can before it runs out. They will be here soon.'

Suddenly I wondered how Ghau had escaped from The Island. He always seemed to be there when I needed him most.

'How did you...?'

He smiled. 'Oh, I came the more ... usual way, once I knew that you and Saa had jumped.' He looked grim. 'When Sharon told me, there seemed no point in staying on that damn lump of rock. I left with the boat that had come to take us.'

He didn't say any more, and I thought how I would have felt if I had been the one on the boat ... not knowing, thinking I had lost everything.

Maybe he knew what I was thinking.

'But my heart told me that you were not gone, not dead. So I searched the high-water mark where the tide had thrown its wreckage, where broken things are left behind by the water. I found Saa. And then I found you. And you were not broken. You are strong.'

And in his words were a promise.

Suddenly, I was overcome with a great tiredness that seemed to come from my soul, and my eyes began to close.

Ghau covered me with dry grass and herbs he had gathered at the place where beach meets land, and I slept close to Saa, my arm over her neck, while he guarded us, and we waited for the men to come in trucks to get us.

I dreamed again – dreams of a new time that was coming. I dreamed of the time when my people – and Ghau's people, and the other people of the rain – would join hands together and build our world again. I dreamed of Lion running, running in the sun. I dreamed of laughter.

I dreamed ... remembering green.

Chapter Fifteen

It was a long way back, a long way. Every step of it was a footstep, a lion-step, a giving up of energy and a giving up of water. But Rain and Ghau did it willingly, and Saa walked with them every print of the way through the dust.

The men had come, grim-faced, in trucks that were rust-red and dying, but they were still able, with much effort and prayer, and swearing, to cross the first, the worst of Drylands, and then of Deadlands. Rain shuddered to see it. There was no drop, no drip, only a memory of water – and that long gone. She huddled in her woollen shawl, and thought: what will become of this place?

Ghau only looked forward. Sometimes Rain wondered if he remembered her at all. He was focused on a time that was to come.

As for Saa – Saa conserved. That was the word for what she did, resting and storing her energy, as if she knew how much she would be needed, how much it would cost in the end. And they travelled and travelled, and the land slowly changed, until there was hope again in their hearts, and Rain slowly unfurled herself from her cloak of wool and despair, and smiled.

And then came a day when wild, white clouds boiled in high skies and the land whispered of rain, and there was a quiet in the land.

'Rain,' Ghau said softly. 'I am going.'

She knew that.

'I know,' she said. And he took her hand in his and looked forward, as he had done through all this journey.

'I will come back,' he said.

'I know,' she answered.

And it was quick and clean, and Ghau was gone, and his footsteps in the dust were blown away as she watched, as she stood with her hand on Lion, her heart still.

And the Travellers came who had been summoned, and they were no longer the enemy, but people who would take her home. They did not smile (Travellers never do), but they respected her and were quiet, and did not speak of the things that were in their hearts or the things they imagined were in hers.

And Rain came home.

LESLEY BEAKE has written over 60 books
for children and young adults. Her international
awards include a Children's Book of Note and
ALA Best Book for Young Adults for *Song of Be,*
and she has been nominated for both the Hans
Christian Andersen and the Astrid Lindgren Awards.
Her first book for Frances Lincoln was the
highly-acclaimed picture book *Home Now*,
illustrated by Karin Littlewood. Lesley lives
in Simon's Town, near Cape Town,
South Africa.